Sheep Blast Off !

Sheep Blast Off!

Written *by* **Nancy Shaw**

Illustrated *by* **Margot Apple**

sandpiper

Houghton Mifflin Harcourt
Boston New York

To Kathy, Jim, Elly, Lotfi, Jim, and Marnie   –N.S.

For Grayson and Ella Rizzi and cousin Francis   –M.A.

Text copyright © 2008 by Nancy Shaw
Illustrations copyright © 2008 by Margot Apple

All rights reserved. Published in the United States by Sandpiper, an imprint of Houghton Mifflin Harcourt
Publishing Company. Originally published in hardcover in the United States by Houghton Mifflin Company,
an imprint of Houghton Mifflin Harcourt Publishing Company, 2008.

Sandpiper and the Sandpiper logo are trademarks of Houghton Mifflin Harcourt Publishing Company.

For information about permission to reproduce selections from this book, write to Permissions,
Houghton Mifflin Harcourt Publishing Company, 215 Park Avenue South, New York, New York 10003.

www.hmhbooks.com

The text of this book is set in Garamond.
The illustrations are colored pencil.

The Library of Congress has cataloged the hardcover edition as follows:

Library of Congress Catalog Number 2007034290

ISBN: 978-0-618-13168-6 hardcover
ISBN: 978-0-547-52025-4 paperback

Printed in China
LEO 10 9 8 7 6 5 4 3 2
4500289900

Sheep see a shape in the mist, by a tree.

Something has landed! What can it be?

Sheep snoop. Sheep explore.

Sheep climb through the spaceship door.

Sheep stumble. Sheep bumble.

Engines slowly start to rumble.

They grab a knob. It seals the door.

Lights come on. Engines roar.

Everyone gets into gear.
They blast right through
the stratosphere.

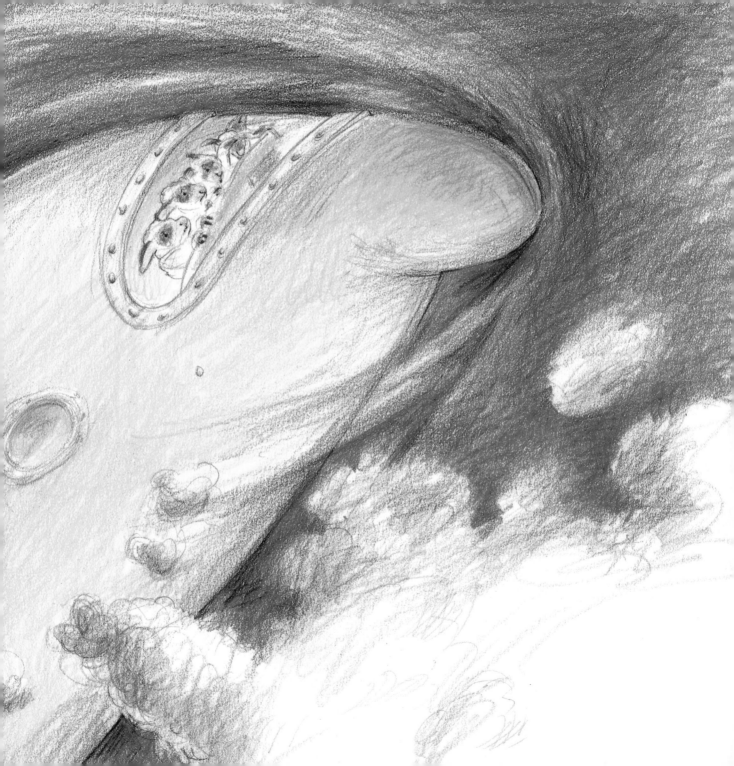

Around the world
the rocket zips.
Weightless sheep
do jumps and flips.

What's that thump? They hit the deck.

Two sheep float
outside to check.

There's just a scratch.

It looks okay.

Back through the hatch—

they're on their way.

They tinker with the main controls.

The rocket lurches, swoops, and rolls.

Lights flash.

Computers beep.

Blaring sirens scare the sheep.

Sheep panic. Sheep guess.

Which button should they press?

Autopilot! That's the one!

Leaving orbit! Nicely done!

Prepare for touchdown!

Home at last!

Rocket sheep have had a blast.